The Worthwhile Flux

The Worthwhile Flux

COREY FROST

conundrum press • montreal

© 2004 Corey Frost
Edited by Andy Brown
Design by Möbius Dick
Photos by Corey Frost
See page 141 for complete credits

Library and Archives Canada Cataloguing in Publication

Frost, Corey
    The worthwhile flux / Corey Frost.

Short stories.
ISBN 1-894994-06-X

    I. Title.

PS8561.R66W67 2004   C813'.54   C2004-904291-2

Dépot Legal, Bibliothèque nationale du Québec
Printed in Quebec on 100% recycled paper
First Edition

conundrum press
PO Box 55003, CSP Fairmount
Montreal, Quebec, H2T 3E2, Canada
conpress@ican.net   http://home.ican.net/~conpress

The publisher wishes to acknowledge the financial assistance of
the Canada Council for the Arts toward its publishing program,
including the production of this book.

**Canada Council
for the Arts**   **Conseil des Arts
du Canada**

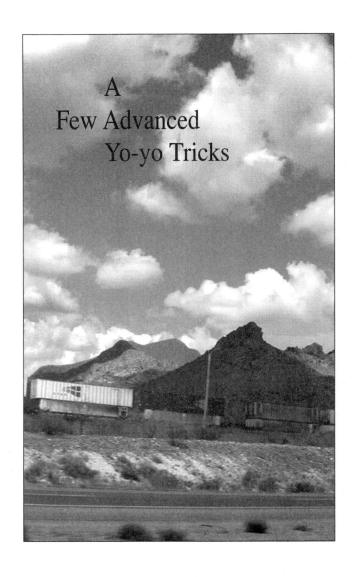

A
Few Advanced
Yo-yo Tricks

Two people are travelling on a train.
Suddenly there is an accident.

But they're both okay.

A nuclear device is stolen from a former Soviet
Republic, but it is soon recovered.

A little girl inherits a lot of money, and that makes her happy. However she soon spends it all, and then she is unhappy. Then the girl makes a friend, and she is happy again. Then her friend goes away, and she is unhappy. Her friend comes back, so she is happy. But the friend has only come back to get his CDs, so the girl is unhappy again. A man has a fox, a goose, and a box of graham crackers. And then, he doesn't. There's only one thing worse than a giraffe with a sore throat. This is a nice place you've got here.

Once there was a little girl, and she was very happy. Suddenly, she acquired supernatural powers. But with great power comes great responsibility, and this caused the girl anxiety and made her unhappy. So she relinquished her powers, and became a normal girl again, and she was happy. I broke my leg in two places so the doctor told me to stop going to those places.

But being a normal little girl was also very stressful, for reasons she couldn't yet understand, and it made her unhappy once again. She decided what she wanted to do with her life, and the decision made her happy. Then she learned that she had no talent for the thing she had decided to do, so she was unhappy. The next time you're on a bus, try this little trick. What's the worst that could happen?

But she soon finds a job working with computers, and it pays enough that she can live in a comfortable apartment and save enough money for a trip to New Orleans, and she is happy. However the job is mind-numbing and soul-destroying, and that makes her unhappy. Dying is the last thing I want to do. Then she finds that she really enjoys watching light romantic comedy films, and watching them makes her happy. But she has a film student acquaintance who has more sophisticated tastes and he relentlessly makes fun of these movies and always ruins it for her. Which makes her unhappy. What's wrong with this picture?

Does the name Pavlov ring a bell? Once there was a girl who read a book, which she really liked and which was meaningful to her, and that made her happy. But then a sequel came out, and then the book was made into a TV series, peppered with advertising aimed squarely in the girl's demographic direction, and she realized that her experience with the book had been in no way unique, and the thought that she could be so easily niche marketed made her feel queasy, and then she was very unhappy.

I'm angry and tired because people keep explaining things to me which are painfully obvious. Sometimes, people will think someone is naïve or deluded, when really that person is simply nurturing a healthy love of contradiction. Sometimes, people will mistake abject longing for despair. But can you blame them? The weather is getting milder, don't you think?

Then she thought she would have a child, and dreams of raising a little girl of her own made her happy. But then she read the statistics on the percentage of children taking Ritalin or Prozac or other psycho-therapeutic drugs, and she read an article about world overpopulation and the selfishness of North Americans who have children only to assuage their dissatisfaction with their own lives. And she decided not to have a child after all. And this made her unhappy. Then she got some goldfish, which made her happy.

[Musical interlude...]

But they died, which made her unhappy. Let's call it a day. I am very tired and I think we have covered the main points on the agenda.

She started seeing a therapist, who helped her put things in perspective, and this made her happy. But then the therapist wanted to sleep with her, and when the girl demurred the therapist said they had accomplished all that they could accomplish unless she was willing to take it to the next level, and cancelled all further appointments, and that made her unhappy. Everyone is conditioned to expect meanings, even though everyone knows they're worthless because there are already too many on the market. Everything is available. Everything is just fine. Everything is ruined. Everything is going exactly according to plan. Everything must go. Some things have lost their taste. I want mint to be exciting again.

Then one day she was in the park, sitting on a bench and eating a lunch that she had made for herself, when a man she did not know, an older man, walked up to her, handed her a piece of paper, and walked away. Everyone is sitting out in the cafés, like it was summer. Try not to think about it, because as soon as you do, it usually disappears. On the paper was a note. It said, I've dreamed of your face. Have a nice day. At first the girl found it sappy, and then creepy, and she was angry at the man, and she didn't want to be made happy by this anonymous note, but she couldn't help it, and eventually she realized it did make her happy. All that afternoon at work she was happy, and she decided to walk home rather than take the bus, and all the way home she was happy. How do you know you'll be able to use your words when you really need to? All the used-up dirty snow is crumpled on the sidewalk like a Kleenex. When the girl got home, she shut the door and looked at her face in the mirror and at first she did believe it. But then she faltered, and her belief in what the note had said went away. This made her sad. The passengers on an airliner are waiting for the pilot to arrive. The plane is sitting on the runway. They are waiting and waiting.

Everyone wonders what's going on.

Then the pilot arrives, and the plane leaves. For a long time not much happens. The girl feels neither happy nor unhappy. She has no opinion one way or the other. Take me with you. I have the gift of prophecy. You never know, I could be very valuable to you. I've been studying the stars. This one's called "Splitting the atom." It's the best one.

Summer Plum
(Winter Version)

I was about seven years old, and it was summer. Our rabbits had miraculously survived another winter. I gave them some carrots to munch on, and then I went back inside. My mother was making squares for fellowship group at the church. On the table there was an open bag of shredded coconut, which I had never seen before. What's this? I asked. It's coconut, she said. Can I have some? Yes, she said, but it won't make you fly. Apparently when she was a kid her older sisters had convinced her that if you ate enough coconut you would be able to fly, but it hadn't worked. She had eaten so much she got sick, and then she got her head stuck in a milkcan. Her skepticism didn't deter me from trying, though, so I took the bag out on the front steps and started eating it. I can't believe how lucky I am, I thought to myself. Soon I'll be flying.

After a few handfuls I went and stood in the driveway and waited for something to happen. I didn't wave my arms or anything; I just stood there in my swimming trunks with my face turned straight up to the sky. I was astonished. The sky was so blue that I completely forgot what I was doing, and my mind started to wander. I hope I will be comfortable in my old age, I thought to myself. Suddenly I realized that the ground was upside down, and I hadn't fallen into the sky only because my feet were stuck to the ground. This was my big chance to fly and someone had ruined it by gluing my Keds to the pavement. I don't know who you are, I whispered. But you'll pay for this.

When I graduated from high school I drank a lot of beer. My friends were making my life miserable because my date was shy and she had braces. I had never drunk so much beer in my life. We went to a Chinese restaurant. As we sat down at the table, my head started to spin. What do you know about post-colonialism? I said to the room in general. Then I threw up, and everyone laughed and applauded. Someone up there likes me, I thought to myself. Do you think being happy is the ultimate goal in life, or is it something else?

This is the winter version of a dream I had in the summer. My life can accommodate imagination, but only if it is deprived of other things, like food, sleep, and comfortable clothing. This is the story of my life, as experienced by other people. Personally, I've never been anywhere, or seen anything. I'd like to stretch my legs someday. I guess I'm what you'd call the travelling type. I'm a restless soul. None of my family are interested in travel, so obviously it's not hereditary. I'd like to go someplace where real coconuts fall from trees; I'd like to see how that would taste. It's just, I've never had the chance to develop my travelling abilities. The world is always either too big or too small. That's why I've never been able to satisfy my deepest longings. It's because the world is the wrong size.

You are the wind. I am the snowbank.

You are the moon. I am the rabbits
buried under the snowbank.

You are the sun. I am the toolshed.

I can see humanity from here. Or at
least, I can see parts of it.

This is the winter version of a story I was supposed to tell you in the summer. One day, for diverse reasons, I suddenly wanted to eat a plum. And so what do you think I do? Do I go to the grocery store and buy a plum and bring it home and eat it, like any normal civilized person? Yes, I do. Yes I do. It's just like they always say. There I am, with my plum, which I have brought home along with all my other things. On the one hand I have my things: you know, my extension cord, my cheese grater, my coat hangers, my Vic-20, my Hi-Tecpoint V5 Extra Fine, my sofa, my UHU Stic, and so on, and then I have this plum. The plum is breathtakingly nice. It's round and purple and, above all, plump. I can't believe how lucky I am, I think to myself. Where did this plum come from? Where did my staggering good fortune come from? Am I living in some fantastical twenty-first-century golden age, when I can just buy a plum that is nearly as big as my fist and as purple as heck? Yes, I am. I believe this plum is going to turn my life around. Never has any plum been so ripe with great expectations for the future. It is the symbol of everything that is firm and juicy about life. I'm standing in the kitchen, with the plum in my hand, and I say out loud: plump plum. Plump plum. It sounds like a heartbeat. The plum has taken over the duties of my heart. Plump plum.

Have you ever lived through a devastating personal tragedy? A fire, a coma, a heart attack? I never did find out *who* had glued my sneakers to the ground, but I always suspected. Where *did* this plum come from? Do they *grow* plums around here? This was a plum of uncanny size, that's for sure. No doubt some maniacal, gene-splicing, hormone-shooting, pesticide-spraying Prometheus, some ruthless bucolic usurper of the gods, hell-bent on humongous fruit, had had a hand in this plum. And now that same hand, the same serpentine hand, was proffering the plum to me. The plum had cost $1.60 or some such mind-numbing sum. What am I doing? I panicked. What am I supposed to do with this plump plum?

Plump plum.

It happened that quickly. In a heartbeat. Is eating this piece of fruit morally comparable to eating another piece of fruit? And what about... plastics? Should I use the hot-air dryer or the paper towels? Cruelty-free, or regular? How can I fight today's economic and political trends? Things are getting pretty scary around here. Oh, instigator of invidious fisticuff showdowns. Oh sly mastermind of internecine squabbles, orchestrator of crafty rackets and outrageous blitzkrieg scams. Oh progenitor of disappointing joys! Are you talking to me? Are you listening to me? Are you taking everything and leaving me with nothing but a brown computer and a naïve belief that everyone gets a second chance?

You may wish that none of this had ever happened to you, but trust me. You will walk out of here with a new way of looking at the world. That is, you will look at it as if it had been brought to you at great expense from a distant country, dismantled and with each piece carefully packaged in Styrofoam. There's something I want to know, you will say to your friends. There's a question lingering in the back of my mind, and the answer may be very far away from here. I'm not sure, but I'm willing to take a chance.

The desire that caused me to buy this plum has dissipated, I realize, as I stand in the kitchen with my heart in my hand. And then, for whatever reason, I decide to put the plum in the icebox. It's not that I've consciously decided I'm saving the plum for breakfast, but it's a possibility. I am *probably* saving it for breakfast. Maybe in the morning the plum will be delicious and cold. Who knows? When I get up the next day and go looking for the plum, though, it is still there. I take it out of the icebox. The first thing I ask myself is, how is this a poem? And the next thing I ask myself is, how is this a plum?

5 Minutes with the Communist Manifesto

1 The Communist Manifesto.

7:00 PM ⑩ ⑤ **America's Funniest Home Videos.** Pet tricks. Practical Jokes. Hilarity. Laffs. (Repeat).

8:00 PM ⑩ ⑤ **The Communist Manifesto.** (1948) Karl Marx, Frederick Engels. 150th anniversary version. In the revolution, we will all be DIGITALLY REMASTERED.

8:06 PM ⑩ ⑤ **America's Funniest Home Videos.** Pet tricks. Practical Jokes. Hilarity. Laffs. (Repeat).

8:06 PM ⑩ ⑤ America's Funniest Home

The Communist Manifesto walks slowly out of the water and up the beach. It is absolutely naked. Meanwhile, a spectre is haunting Europe. At the secret headquarters, the workingmen of the world unite. A car chase ensues. The bourgeoisie is trying to escape with the means of production, but the proletariat is following closely in a Lada. As the vehicles careen onto the sidewalk, racks of value-added goods are sent flying. Oranges bouncing everywhere. The fruit vendor stands in the street, waving his fist angrily at the rear window of the vanishing proletariat. The bourgeoisie escapes. But later, the Manifesto, disguised as an electrician, infiltrates the bourgeoisie's private party in an abandoned factory. The bourgeoisie turns out to be extremely difficult to kill, and in the struggle they both fall into a vat of molten steel, which will eventually be used to build a brand new superstructure.

2 Problems for Discussion.

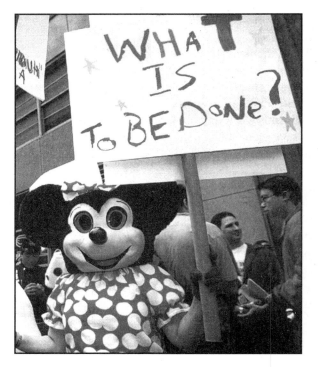

The Communist Manifesto is a document outlining the fundamental tenets of Communism. And, a whole lot more! It is also the opposite. For example, if an assassination occurs on the other side of the world, and the alleged assassins emigrate to this country, then what is my own personal moral imperative? What is this other country? We don't know. We don't know whether it begins with a B or an M. It may begin with some other letter we have never even heard of. What kind of government do they have? Who was this assassinated prime minister? Was he an evil despot who loved his grandchildren? Or was he a revered leader who promoted peace and made the people aware of their own pitiful inadequacies? We don't know. The country is too far away, and there are too many countries, and too many letters of the alphabet to begin with. How can we know these things? What can we do? And I need it on my desk by, like, yesterday.

3 Art and the Manifesto.

The
Manifesto
is always
pathetic.

What, according to the Communist Manifesto, is art? Art is anti-capital. If anti-capital comes into contact with capital, the whole system self-destructs. All art is quite useless, according to Oscar Wilde, not unlike a popsicle stick inscribed with an impossible philosophical query. In a world where capital is matter, then art doesn't matter. The bourgeois artist claims that art is merely the repository of all human knowledge. In fact, art is the suppository of all human knowledge. Art itself, in its unlimited glory, should become a form of art. The French have a word for art. Art should be exercised every day. Take art out for a walk in the park. Throw the frisbee around. If you love art, tie it to a bench and leave it there. Walk away from it, ignoring its pleas. If it escapes by chewing off its own leg and tracks you down, it's yours. If it attacks you, you may legally kill it in self-defense. That's love. That's art.

4 The Dadaist Manifesto of the Communist Manifesto

Feeling removed.

Sadly, today manifestoes are falling out of popularity. A manifesto is rambunctious, and perhaps a tad over-earnest. In art, they have largely been supplanted by autobiography, and by corporate mission statements. It is difficult for the surface and the not-surface to agree, but I assume in my work that the not-surface is actually only superficially removed from the surface. The sub-structure and the super-structure are the same. Whether it is removed above or below the surface is unnecessary.

Q: How would one recognize the Communist Manifesto on the Metro?

A: Really it's about feeling good. Feeling confident. Secure. You have to have a dream. In the beautiful park, in the evening light, a breeze is moving the children in the lake. A frond is waving in the breeze. Think peaceful, think fresh.

5 The Triumph of the Communist Manifesto.

"The Manifesto

has become

an historical document

which we have

no longer

any right

to alter."

Dear Mr. and Mrs. Oscar and Gloria Adams of Swift Margin, Minnesota:

I hear that you have a very smart dog. I hear that he can take the squeezie nozzle of your garden hose in his mouth and that he can spray your two-year-old kid, who is playing in the plastic wading pool, in the face. He knows that he will be rewarded with a Twinkie because this is a very funny thing to do. Clearly, your dog is very intelligent. I'm writing, in fact, because I have something to ask your dog. I want to know if he would mind being featured in a story I'm writing. The story is about the Communist Manifesto. It's a great story with powerful dialogue and international appeal. The ending is a bit anticlimactic. But a dog as smart as yours, Mr. and Mrs. Adams, would really make all the difference.

Yours sincerely,

—K. Marx,
F. Engels,
1872.

In Quotations,
Out of Context

My famous last words are in a small black box. No one has heard them yet. The box is at the bottom of the Atlantic Ocean, about a hundred miles from shore.

"'A quotation within a quotation takes single instead of double quotation marks,' I say.

"'Yes I know,' she answers. 'But what I understood your mother to say was, "Be sure to take enough blankets,"'" you said.

Can I have a dime's worth of bananas? Thank you. Wait. Can I exchange these for a dime's worth of apples? Thank you. Hey, what about the money? The money for what? The money for the apples. But I gave you the bananas for the apples. Well, then, the money for the bananas. But you've still got the bananas. An early morning walk in the woods. A late afternoon walk in the woods. An early morning walk in the city. A late afternoon walk in the city. The railway station just before the train comes in. The railway station just after the train has left. The big parade begins. A fashionable church wedding. Running from an unexpected shower. Mr. Looney Gets a Surprise. An Unusual Experience. The Purloined Letter. The Word that Screamed. The One that Got Away. How to Measure the Height of a Skyscraper, or a Tall Tree. The Disadvantages of Having Ears. A Terribly Strange Bed. The Untangled Tangle. Mr. Onion. The Causes of Dew. Every word of this paragraph was written by someone other than me. Except one.

The subject is copyright. Copyright, an issue of concern to everyone, has become huge. It has bloated beyond recognition and sprawls so far across the thoughtscape of our society that it has become impossible to travel from one idea to another. Toxic waste from copyright has begun to leak into the soil in which ideas are sown, and has even contaminated the drinking water in the well of knowledge. Now its oppressive weight threatens the integrity of the very bedrock of our way of thinking. This could lead, within our lifetimes, to a massive upheaval which would cause billions of dollars' worth of damage to intellectual property. On the bright side, like any immense garbage dump, copyright is a scavenger's paradise. One of the key issues in the debate over copyright is the all-important role of the quotation mark, which some have heralded as a convenient, ergonomical device for dividing copyright into smaller, re-usable pieces. Experts, however, say slow down: "We need to do more studies. These 'quotation marks' may not be safe." What people don't realize, they say, is that quotation is a two-way street. If I quote you, it's exactly the same as if you quote me. As one expert says, why do you think quotation marks are in the shapes of 6s and 9s? It works both ways. It's just a question of who will be the subject and who will be the object.

Instructions for a quotation event:

1. **Quote.**
2. **Unquote.**

The subject is copyright ©. My lawyer says that for a statement to be considered slanderous, it must be proven that it was spoken with malicious intent, and also that it is untrue. I hate my lawyer and I wish him ill. Furthermore, I don't have a lawyer.

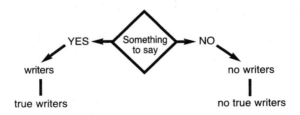

I have a few simple questions and it'll only take a few minutes. The world is made up of two kinds of people. Can I quote you on that? Don't worry, I'm not recording this. I'm concerned that my remarks might be taken OUT OF CONTEXT. Why worry as long as you're telling the truth? Don't answer that. We're not so much interested in whether what you say is true; what matters to us is whether it's authentic. If I may quote the French novelist Alain Robbe-Grillet: "The true writer has nothing to say. What counts is the way he says it." Let's examine why this statement is not "true." First, since there is nothing to say, there can be no writers, and therefore there can be no "true" writers. Furthermore, since writers say nothing, what they say can be neither true nor untrue. The question is rather one of authenticity or inauthenticity. It should be clear, then, that this quotation is not true (coming as it does from a writer), however you may trust that I'm telling the truth when I say that this is an authentic quote from the actual author, Alain Robbe-Grillet.

The authenticity of the quote leads us to several conclusions. First, there are no writers. Rather there are only un-writers, those who untangle truths from what was written before them. If writing is the process of saying nothing, then un-writing works by un-saying all nothings until everything remains. The un-writer must take away all meaninglessness so that what is left, however improbable, must be the meaning. What counts therefore is not the way the writer says it, but the way the *un*-writer *un*-says what was said before. The threads that make up the fabric of the un-written text, of course, are quotations, and the essential un-writing tool is the quotation mark. It is what the un-writer uses to contain and un-say meaninglessness. My grade-eight English teacher said that a direct quotation presents "exactly what was said, in those exact words." And she said it in those exact words.

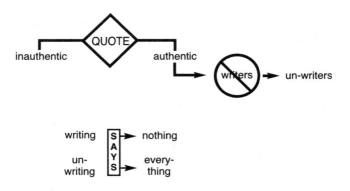

A calm woman's voice that emerges from the dash as you sit in the kidnapper's car says: "Please fasten your seat-belts. I'm not feeling so well." The woman with an artificial leg who walks with the help of crutches and who has just knocked over a flower vase as you are leaving the restaurant says: "Let's dance." The man who insulted you, after you threaten him, says: "I take back everything I said and I give you a full refund. I will not however take back any statements that have been removed from their quotation marks." The ultra-conservative leader of the attempted coup, as he ties up the president with duct tape, says: "You don't have to be crazy to work here, but it helps!" As she lies dying in 1777, in a small cottage near Penzance in Cornwall, Dolly Pentreath, the last surviving speaker of the Cornish language, says: "Ny raf wherthin nefra." Simon, bored with simple hand gestures and drunk with power, says: "Take off your clothes." The anonymous, androgynous voice that sometimes calls me in the middle of the night and whispers questions while I'm half asleep says: "Don't worry. I'm not recording this." The gold-plated record on the Voyager space probe, the farthest human artifact from Earth, says, in Chinese dialect: "Friends of space, how are you all? Have you eaten yet?"

"A quotation," my Sensei tells me, "is like a door into another person's mind." We stand, contemplative, in front of a door. The sign on the door says, *This is not a door*. He continues. "A quotation is not like a jar that you catch words in as if they were grasshoppers." This confuses me, because a memory surfaces from many years ago, of riding in my grandfather's luxury sedan, when the voice in the dash told me that actually, a door *is* a jar.

You (the audience) and I are at cross-purposes. You'd like to unravel the thread of this tissue of quotations, but I'm trying to sew it together to make myself bullet-proof underwear. Are you here for business or pleasure? Or is this some kind of arcane and deeply personal fetishistic ritual? Don't answer that. I'm concerned that my remarks might be taken OUT OF CONTEXT. *This conversation is over! I'm not speaking to you anymore.* Every quotation must be taken out of context, or else it's not a quotation. In order to remain faithful to the spirit of the remark, it becomes necessary to misquote it. Would you say that you've been misquoted? Or would you say, "Eureka"? Anything you say can be used against you. Don't say I didn't tell you not to say I didn't tell you so. As part of my preparations for what will inevitably come next, I'm going to conduct an exhaustive search of all the poems and all the songs and all the speeches and the sermons and stories and jokes and ads and inscriptions—basically, all the quotations—and I'm going to determine what is the one word that has never been used in any of them. Then I'm going to gather everyone I can find together in one room, and I'm going to get myself a microphone and amplifier, and I'm going to use that word. I'm going to use it over and over and over, until it has been so used that no one else will ever be able to use it again. Or until you've had enough.

My famous last words are in a small black box. No one has heard them yet. The box is at the bottom of the Atlantic Ocean, about a hundred miles from shore, and is made of virtually indestructible materials. Seawater, fire, explosions, ice: nothing can penetrate the box, and neither does anything escape. The box is suitable for containing unstable isotopes of plutonium but the only things in it are famous last quotations. Throat-clearings, requests for coffee, the loose ends of epiphany and the punchlines of jokes we told in the last twenty minutes of our lives. We will no doubt be endlessly quoted and re-quoted. The box is equipped with an electronic beacon so that the searchers will always be able to locate the source of the quotations. I'm sure there is no blinking light, but I imagine a small red L.E.D. like the one on my answering machine, letting me know that a message is waiting. They know exactly where the box is, but no one has heard my famous last words, yet. There was a boat out here yesterday, but it was tossed around mercilessly and eventually they had to retreat to the shore. There's a helicopter reconnoitering over the still-undiminished waves now, manned by a coast-guard pilot and co-pilot scanning the water. With his left forefinger and thumb the co-pilot gently bends the mouthpiece of his helmet-radio-headset closer to his face as he leans against the glass. He's trying to get a better look at an unidentifiable piece of flotsam in the water below.

He asks the pilot to turn one more time. The lines of concentration and worry on his face are slowly replaced by a look of incredulous joy and nostalgia. Then, barely audibly, under his breath, in a whisper, he says: "Rosebud." Today is the first day of the rest of your intertextuality. Am I being too direct? Or too indirect? Or is my level of directness just right? What are you waiting for? This is your big chance.

V: The Miniseries

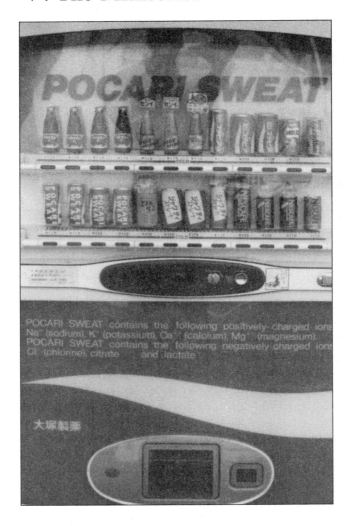

1 Who is Yukio Funai?

M: He is writer... writer and... marketing consultant.
I: Marketing consultant?
M: Yes.
I: Uh-huh.
M: Uh... old man. Bold.
R: Bald.
M: Bald?
I: Bald, yeah.
R: Yes. And... [laughs]
M: Alien! [laughs]

[...]

I: So... seventy percent of young people in the world...
R: Are alien.
I: Are aliens?
M: Yes.
I: Of the three of us then, probably two of us are aliens.
R: That's right. [laughs]
I: But we look like humans, even though we're aliens?
M: Mm. [flipping through dictionary] Uh... pre... con... cep... tion?
I: Because of our preconceptions? We think, humans, humans, humans... so we see humans.
M+R: Yes.
I: Ah.
M: It's not... religion.
I: It's science?
M: Yes.

I'm a visitor in a small town. In two years I've worked my way through the video rental shelves until I come upon *V: The Miniseries*, with Japanese subtitles. (It's a combination of cultural arrogance and a post-modern education that allows me to find this interesting.)

I'm the first to realize that The Invaders are among us. Our preconceptions cause us to mistake ourselves for humans, until we turn out to be lizards, or communists. What gives us away finally is our eyes. They're green, or on stalks, or we can see 180 degrees like a chameleon. Children aren't confused by our disguises. They draw my Japanese-American friend with blond hair and blue eyes like the *gaijin* that she is. And they interrogate me: why are my eyes a different colour from hers, since I'm a *gaijin* too? The first episode ends with everyone submitting to retina scans.

Yours are green,
Greener than I've ever seen...

2 We Are a Library

I: What is the difference? Between an alien and a human?
R: Uh... Aliens have... love.
I: Love?
R: Yes, yes. Love. Don't... don't have... eggos?
I: Aliens don't have Eggos?
R+M: Yes.
(Pause.)
I: Egos. Aliens don't have egos.

What we are afraid of is here to save us, of course, save us from ourselves, make us fall in love with ourselves, fall in love with abduction, invasion, colonization, redemption. Under hypnosis I remember my own abduction, which explains why I'm singing Okinawan folk songs.

> *Yours are brown,*
> *browner than I've ever found...*

M: Our earth is... material for... expi... experiment.
I: What kind of experiment?
R: Li... eh, to... library is... us.
I: Us? We are a library?
R: Yes. Intelligence is... is light.
I: Uh-huh. And no intelligence is...
R: Yes...
I: Dark?
R: Yes. Dark. Yes yes yes.

The plot thickens and reluctantly we admit that what the alien really wants is not the rough sex or the mutilated cattle, but knowledge, the consolidation of the light and the dark perhaps, understanding of the world, or the universe—and we are like the infinite library of Borges. The human genome mapping project is like a giant card catalogue. (*Quiet please, someone may be trying to read...*

3 Like an Otherworldly Dream

In the last episode I have a close encounter with a child who points at me and yells across the street: "*Gaijin da!*"

I gently correct him: "*Chigau. Uchujin desu.*" I am not a foreigner. I am an alien. You are not dressed like an alien, he points out contemptuously. I may look remarkably human, but that is because perception and genetics operate in stranger ways than you can imagine. My name is Alphonse Le Chevalier and I have five spleens, extraordinarily long intestines, and miraculous powers, including translation. My heart has two hundred chambers instead of your four, and this has allowed me to achieve a state of perfect love and peace. I will want to teach this to you, as well, but you will be too distracted. By the shade of my irises. And the length of my eyelashes. The story will end in tragedy.

M: The Earth now… doesn't have… it has only
darkness.
I: Ah. Only darkness.
M: Yes.
R: Very sad. [laughs]
I: So it's very sad.
M: Yeah. [laughs]
R: [laughing]
I: No, it's very sad that the Earth has no intelligence.

Yours are green,
Greener than I've ever seen.
Like an otherworldly dream
Mine are brown and yours are green.

Yours are brown,
Browner than I've ever found.
Like a saucer touching down
Mine are green and yours are brown.

Everything I Know
About Aphids

Okay now this may hurt a little. I want you to tell me when it hurts okay can you do that? Alright. Does it hurt when I do this? No. Does it hurt now? No it's fine. What about if I do this? No. It doesn't hurt? No. Can you feel this? I don't feel anything. Okay I'm going to do something else that will hurt more but it'll only last a second. Okay? Alright. Are you ready? Yes. Did it hurt? No. Okay I'm going to do it again except harder. Did it hurt? ... No. No, I didn't feel anything at all. I feel perfectly fine. Am I normal?

This is not a joke but it is going to sound like one at first. A Nobel-prize-winning physicist, a world-renowned countertenor, the prime minister of an industrialized country, and the Pope are all on a plane with you. The plane is going to crash and everyone will die. Alright. There is one parachute. Alright. Tell me what colour is the parachute. Well. Do you know, well, I think I know about 100 times more of people whom I've never met than names of people I actually know. I don't like electricity. I'm trying to be stylish without actually being in style. I'm easy-going. I'm like a mushroom raised in captivity. I am surrounded by shit and darkness and I thrive on it. I think that maybe, it might just be possible that conceivably, perhaps, I need to do something new with my hair.

I'm a nebulous figure. I'm as nebulous as a commercial for mutual funds. I'm as dubious as a first-time test-market. I'm as sad as a toothbrush. The residues of my dreams are probably the most valuable things I have right now. Recently I purchased a ham-radio but I don't know how to use it or even what it is for. I believe in freedom, sure, who doesn't? This country of ours is a place where we can look into one another's hearts and dreams. When is a good time to call? I'm as peaceful as a continental shelf. I'm as ambitious as a coffee franchise. I'm learning to laugh at myself, even though I'm not funny. I voluntarily appear in advertisements for my favourite products. I send fan mail to the people who write headlines. Those things might be funny. Not funny funny, but not funny strange either. Somewhere in between.

I'm as confident as an American Express card. However, I'm as troubled as an underwater toilet. I have an item at home. It's my favourite item. This item uses zero K of disk space. I believe what you were saying earlier, that in the new world order, every night will be cheap night. There's a good statistical probability that the vast majority of people I've never met are also people you've never met. I am going to give you my opinion of those people. I'm as eloquent as a Seventh-Day Adventist past his expiration date. Humans are people who like people who are more beautiful than they are. I'm as evolved as a genetically-altered peach. I'm like a Japanese animé version of myself, except not as cheerful. Was it Descartes? Or was it Spinoza? I know it wasn't Hegel, but it might have been Heidegger. I'm as post-traumatic as a standardized test score. I'm as uncertain as a ruble. I'm like a cross between serendipity and silly putty. I'm as mawkish as a Jello tree. I may not be as funny as a joke, but nevertheless, I am. The best thing for us to do right now is to keep our heads. We can get through this if we act in a civilized manner. Here's my impression of John Hinckly Jr.

I'm as calm as fallout. I'm as unified as a Cartesian rummage sale. It's as if I'm running my own talk show on my own network, with my own questions and myself as a guest and an audience made up of me. I'm as angry as transvestite dwarves and the women who love them. I'm as useful as a desktop sewage treatment plant. It's as if the linguistic medium is actually a few sizes too large or too small. I'm as sincere as a flesh-eating bacteria. I'm as user-friendly as an automatic sledge-hammer. I'm like a fast-acting autonomous anti-depressant with nanotechnology. It's as if the guy in front of the bank is begging a question. Does it mean what it really means, or does it mean what people think it means? I'm as wise as a Papal bull in a china shop. It's as if you took all of the veins and arteries in your body, and all the veins and arteries in my body, and all your nerves, and all my nerves, and the nerves and arteries and veins of all the people you know and all the arteries and veins and nerves of all the people on Earth, and laid them end to end.

I'm as excited as a big red button. I'm like the fly on the windshield of an accelerating car. I'm like the driver who is trying to shake the fly off the windshield. I'm like the driver's son in the back seat who is hoping that the fly can hold on. I'm like, don't ask, don't tell. And you're like, oh you say that now. And I'm like, what are you talking about. And you're like, here we go again. I'm like a futurologist who can't stop thinking about the past. I'm like an adult who still gets tears in his eyes when he sees snow falling. I'm an adult, like every other person on the planet. I can identify the parts of any sentence, what tense it is in, and what mood. This is the subject, this is the verb. There are only two tenses in English: there is no future tense, only future forms. The mood is always the same too. My mood is always the same. It's as if someone forgot about theme, characterization, and plot. I'm as ironic as a hay ride.

Everything I know about aphids. I know everything about aphids. Aphids I know everything about. I know about everything, *aphids*. I'm as wired as a potato in a grade 9 science fair project. I'm as angst-ridden as a good ethnic cleansing. I'm as sequential as the next guy. I can be as bright as gingham or as dumb as chintz. The future is not going to sound like a joke for the first few years, but it is. I have the corporate media oligarchy in my pocket and I intend to use it to make myself a celebrity and make everyone I know into glorified servants and whores. When's the last time we did something together, as a family? What you are going to experience represents the artistic vision of its sole creator, the author, and can not be quoted, copied, reproduced, re-interpreted, violated, mutilated, or misunderstood in whole or in part without express written consent. By accepting these terms you waive all recourse to objection, legal or otherwise. Yes, I accept these terms. I am now ready to enter the twenty-first century. No, I do not accept these terms. I will leave immediately and renounce all further interest in this century or in any other century which may come after it.

My relationship to the world is like that of an aphid. I exist by sucking up everything I can, and then I am milked by a highly organized colony of social insects. I need a bigger mental environment. Fuck you Fred Phelps and everything you stand for. These fascinating insects come in many shapes and colours. There are many kinds of aphids and they all have legs. Aphids come in many varieties and they all have shapes and colours. Also, all the aphids are very small. Does it hurt yet? Yes, now it's starting to hurt a little bit. Thank you.

5 Minutes with the Global Economy

Two people are travelling on a plane. One turns to the other. He is of the opinion, it seems, that the North-South divide could be resolved if the labour markets were completely liberalized so that skilled workers could migrate to developed countries, work, and send money home to their families. The second traveller considers this carefully. Finally he turns to the first traveller. "I am in a lot of pain," he says. The plane continues on its route between Heathrow and Moscow. The first traveller, whose name is Alum, is going home to Bangladesh. The second traveller isn't sure where he is going. But only in a figurative sense, of course. He knows the plane is going to Moscow. In reality, if he somehow found himself on a plane without knowing its destination, he would certainly ask someone. I know, because that second traveller was me.

This will only take a few minutes. I'm calling on behalf of the global economy. Your level of satisfaction with the global economy can be best described as? Very satisfied, satisfied, indifferent, unsatisfied, very unsatisfied. Your level of success in the global economy can be best described as? I am unsuccessful and unpopular; I am able to feed my family rice once a day as long as my eight children work in the sweatshops; I have more than one t-shirt and I once tasted a bottle of Coca-Cola; I can read and some of my teeth are intact; I just bought a new computer that talks to me; I am the dictator of an oil-rich country and I am about to purchase my first nuclear weapon. Most of the time you feel? Very happy, happy, somewhat happy, neutral, unhappy, very unhappy, extremely unhappy, miserable, absolutely miserable, resigned to a life of hardship and pain in the hope that I will come back as something better. What new products would you like to see the global economy produce which would make your life complete, and how would you feel about the global economy being available 24 hours a day on the internet? I'm not sure I understand what I'm being asked. Let me explain.

Let me put it this way. During the Napoleonic Wars, the British fleet shut off the West Indies sugar supply from the French. At the behest of Napoleon, French botanists developed the sugar beet into a satisfactory source of sugar, and Continental Europe became nearly independent of the West Indies. What happened to the West Indies sugar plantations, which had been set up by Europeans? Well, that's a good question. So what am I saying? Well, sometimes I feel that you are Europe and I am the West Indies. Do you see what I am getting at? You hold the power in this relationship right now. But whatever net benefit you're accruing, there is an equal and opposite benefit for me in providing it to you. Need creates reciprocal need, and neither of us can ever attain independence without independence for the other. I just want to know how much you'll give me, to do that thing that you like me to do. I want to know how much you're willing to pay.

In telling the real story of the global economy, I have adhered closely to fact, and therefore have been obliged occasionally to use strong and coarse expressions, which may be painful to nice feelings, for which I apologize. I am unwilling to present this narrative without a few words in explanation of my rationale. There have been so many stories told about the global economy that I should think it unjustifiable in me to add another story to the vast number already in existence without being able to give reasons in some measure warranting me in so doing. My reasons, unfortunately, are ignoble. While this is the true story of the global economy, it is also, I confess, a repressed tantrum. My desire—nay, my compulsion—that it be told is a measure of my maladjustment as a participant in the prosperity of our times. In preparing this narrative, I have regretfully incorporated impressions made upon me by puerile discontent. I have reserved more sensible views, suggested by subsequent reflection, for my concluding remarks, to which I now respectfully call your attention.

Today is another beautiful day. As I step from my back porch into the garden, a chorus of songbirds heralds the arrival of the glorious dawn. The sky is an immaculate, limpid blue. Fanciful insects busy themselves with their pollen-carrying duties amidst the flowerbeds, while the scent of honeysuckle wafts into the yard on a gentle breeze. This day has just been imported from Saipan, in the Northern Mariana Islands, where the assembly workers do quality work at very reasonable rates. Best of all, not a penny of excise tax was paid on it. Ahh. I almost catch the scent of bougainvillaea. The global economy is operating noiselessly and perfectly, just beyond those trees over there. My new computer has a 1.5 GHz processor, 256 MB RAM, 80 Gig hard drive, DVD-R, ACI Rage pro graphics card with 64 MB VRAM, Firewire, USB, ethernet, and wireless capability. I have no idea where it is.

A Farewell
to Q

The truth is, we never appreciated you enough. Without a
sound of your own, you were a strangely foreign charac-
ter, usually perched at the end of Arabic or third-from-last
in French. You were the loser in the alphabetic popularity
contest—which, paradoxically, was the measure of your
worth in Scrabble. But even then you were a blessing and
a curse: cheered on your arrival, you would end up being
dumped.

Farewell, coyly elusive companion of U and I! Farewell, ossified vowel with the vestigial tail! We never knew how much we loved you, and once you are gone we'll never know why we needed you in the first place.

Hardly anyone is happy. It's heartening to be in the streets with my affinity group, handkerchief over my mouth, but next year I know we'll find something else to agitate against, not because we are constitutionally so disposed, but because the various affronts of this unromantic world are constantly being re-served to us like dicey leftovers. Park of King's Wife is sympathetically unhelpful. "These protests are touching but futile," insist our leaders in answer to interrogatives. "It's like protesting Spring, or Globalization."

The effects are widespread.[1] Ecuador will have a new capital, as will Nunavut. A certain sheikdom on the Persian Gulf will cease to exist, and a nearby born-again democracy will be given a less barbaric name—although the occupying army will still face an imbroglio.[2] Corporate identities may be re-envisioned to emulate forward-thinking businesses like Kwik-Kopy. And of course an entire province will disappear, referendum or no. Eventually we will resign ourselves to these changes.[3]

[1] But not *ubiquitous*. [2] But not a *quagmire*. [3] But never *acquiesce*.

What will the future be like? The British will have to start lining up for things. Magazines and literary reviews will appear triennially, or bimonthly, or work out some other arrangement. We will go back to using "barbecue" sauce, while gays, lesbians, bisexuals and transgender persons will go back to being odd, unnatural, or eccentric. At a loss for things to say, we will cite the words of others. "Liberty, fraternity, and everyone being treated the same," will be the motto of our times. The streets before dawn will be silent.

In New York, the subway is losing the line whose name I came to love, the one I used to sleep with. That year the steel-blue bridge from Chinatown to Dumbo arched above me and I kept the window open, letting in the shimmer and noise and the East River's West Nile mosquitoes. The subway rattled over the bridge, sparks falling like disappearing hail. At first it kept me awake, then it put me to sleep, an embarrassingly real train entering the intangible tunnels of my dreams.

Last night was its final run, down a track that disappears under the sand at Brighton Beach. I didn't attend the wake, but I saw it pass, late at night, underground. As I leaned against the dark window of another train, under another letter, occupied with my own portion of the sadness we all share, it flashed into sight: illegally-opened windows trailing yellow police tape, mourners swinging from the straps and slam-dancing in the aisles or snogging between the cars. Confetti swirled as though in a snow-globe, and people were getting undressed. Pressed against one corner of one window was the face of a young woman, lost in thought like me.

As our trains ran side-by-side, into the station, we held one another's gaze, from opposite sides of the platform. Our eyes remained locked when the doors slid open and people burst out, dashing from one car to another. We sat, momentarily, after the revellers scrambled inside, and the person in the other window beckoned. For a long, anxious minute I was undecided, but then I leaped out, doors sliding shut behind me. I had waited too long, though. As I crossed the platform, her doors closed and she left for the ocean without me. It was there on a subway platform, after watching her solemn face move away, that I said my final goodbye to my favourite letter.

Those who will read these words ages hence will perhaps be unaware that a letter was even lost, for they will not need it. History may neglect that there ever were things that it stood for: such and such a dance, such a fruit, such a bird, such a theory, such a game, such a dumpling, such a feeling. They will no longer know of such things, but such things do exist, and for the time being at least I can utter their names: *quadrille, quince, quail, quantum, quoits, quenelle, queasiness.*

I knew you well, Q. I knew you like I'd know a lover's name, but I loved you without realizing that I did. They say that in the future it will be worse. People will still love, but they will only be able to love what they've never heard of, what they don't even know exists. It's sad, but it's how things are.

Acadian Bus Lines

1 January. I leave Snail Cove, leave Bottom River, leave the island where a huge bridge is being built with a brain the size of a pea. I arrive in Moncton, which has always been extinct. That makes it more magnetic, makes me want to record it on a four-track tape in the basement, lay down the bones, play it over and over until it becomes meaningless. I switch buses there: in the sky, grey and wet clouds, like a doormat. The NB Power tower looks like a huge worn-out toilet brush sticking straight up from the bowl. Moncton is the bowl.

I get on the bus. You're not beside me, but I still pretend you are. You don't even know I'm coming to see you. You invited me but you'd be angry if you knew. All the people on the bus would be angry. So I sit up front under a glowing sign that says Montreal backwards. You sit by the window — which is another island — we squeeze each other's arms in anticipation. On the other side the bus interior floats along the roadside. Backwards versions of you and I lean forward and wave, legs melting into the snowbanks. They wait for us to curl up and sleep, then quietly slip their hands into each other's pants.

Fredericton. I stretch and get off, on, everything glazed with ice, the moon out, in good spirits. Back on the bus, I start talking to you about you, explain with uncharacteristic candour my feelings, make you promise not to tell. You reveal some embarrassing stories from your childhood. You think it's fun, you want to call you. In an Irving station in Edmunston we huddle around a receiver. You answer, we laugh, you pretend we're still on the island but I'm not, you've never left. Nothing suspicious here.

Our reflections have fallen asleep and I've sunk into reflective silence. What's wrong? I'm sorry, I'm having a fantastic time on this highway. It's like a Möbius strip. You confuse me, you're far away. You talk about surprising you: we'll go get me first, go over all together or maybe wait, surprise me too. I promise I'll act surprised. But I can't wait so I leave you, go directly to your bed, creep in, wait, but you've never left.

The bus arrives. You come in, I leap out of bed, hug you, put down my bags. It's good to be back. Am I ever surprised to see you, you tell me. You've never left the island though, you shrug, I remember I promised to be surprised. I've made it this far—Rivière du Loup—where we make a quick call, say, sorry, can't come surprise you, get back on the bus in the opposite direction. We're tired of the shape of the seats. I glance out the window: our reflections have gone away somewhere. Moncton is flushed in a pale winter dawn. The drained Petitcodiac looks backed-up and brown.

On the boat I take you out on deck to lean over the railing. We watch the sun surface like a peach in thick syrup. You don't feel well. I'm not on the island, you say, I'm somewhere else, as far as you know, as far as you know how. You look down at the churning ice, holding your stomach. I sigh, watch the snow on the cliffs. Your new place is far, I'll never find a bus—Japan—another island, a whole archipelago. To build the bridge will take another three years.

In the pocket of a seat we have a pamphlet, a blue map, straight space-age coastlines, passenger coaches on each city. A yellow line connects the dots like a laser beam. You rest your head on my arm and trace the lines with your finger, you trace the line of your escape off the edge, across my arm. On the glass you leave wet tracks in the dirty steam, through which I see muddy fields, whimsical mailboxes. You say, please stop following me.

We take the rest of the bus ride to about where I started. I'm still confused, you're asleep in my lap, I have to carry you off, set you on the shoulder. I don't know what to do or don't want to wake you, ask. You're on the island, asleep on the side of the highway. As if you stop moving when I stop chasing, when I run out of things to say. It's not my story that moves you. It's not me that moves you.

2 Stop chasing when I run out. I don't know what to do or don't. About where I started I'm still confused. Whimsical mailboxes you say please stop. Like a laser beam you rest your head. In the pocket of a seat we have.

Well I'm not on the island. Surprised I've made it this far. Go directly to your bed creep. Surprise me too I promise I'll act surprised. I stretch and get off on everything. The snowbanks they wait for us. You'd be angry if you knew all the people. I still pretend you are you. Until it becomes meaningless I switch buses. With a brain the size of a pea I arrive in Moncton.

3 I switch buses with a brain the size of a pea. I still pretend you are you until it becomes meaningless. For us you'd be angry if you knew. Bed creep surprise. Well I'm not. You say please stop like a laser beam. I'm still confused. Whimsical. When I run out I don't know what.

4 Surprise well I'm not you. It becomes meaningless for us. With a brain the size of a pea I still pretend.

Stories That Don't
Explain Anything

When I was six, I got my first bicycle. It was white, with a fat back tire and a banana seat and chopper handlebars. Recently, I went to a museum, and the bicycle was there. I didn't have much money, so I sold my car and returned home on foot, buying a saw along the way. It was cold in my room. I put on a sweater and had a big cup of coffee, and then I had a big glass of water, although I shouldn't have. They say that after Genghis Khan was finished killing and pillaging, he would have a bowl of soup. I had soup just the other day.

One day I went to La Ronde, where that guy works, with the mohawk. When I got back, your sister had been swimming in the pool, for at least two hours. I had to take an aspirin for my head—when I was young, I couldn't take aspirin. I took a shower, but I had the same problem. Last year, I went to Hungary. One is not supposed to clink beer glasses there. In Japan, you shouldn't stand your chopsticks in your rice. Every place has its own customs. Next month I'm going to Johannesburg and my friend told me not to get out of the car. Last night, while I slept, I spoke.

I was playing hockey and during the game, I got hurt. My friend put me in an ambulance and gave me his camera. But I realized that I had forgotten my health insurance card. "I'll call my mother," I told him. She isn't going to be happy when I tell her you don't want to have children. My friend makes noise when he eats. Moreover, he makes noise while walking. People across the street look at him as if they are seeing a monster.

The other day my neighbour was working in his backyard. He obviously wanted to see what I was doing. I think he was really surprised, although there was no reason to be. After that, he couldn't go to the store, because his car was being repaired, so he practiced a few moves he was working on. He believes that if he keeps practicing, he will succeed. But he's not really talented. Two years ago, he was doing some other activity because he thought it would be more fun. However, with the passing of time I guess he found that it was no longer fun.

My family was laughing a lot. Suddenly, I stood up and I apologized to my mother, because I had damaged her knitting equipment and it couldn't be repaired. Apologizing always makes me angry. I left the house and made for the hills. I ran and ran, chased by a pack of dogs. When I climbed a tree they forgot about me and ran off into a field. They nipped at each other's heels and jumped and nibbled on grass and barked for a long time.

John was lying on his bed, remembering what he'd done. In his hand he was holding a pistol, and he was wondering what he should do now. He began to pray. He didn't know any prayers. He began to cry. Everyone at the wedding had been laughing. Would the marriage be a happy one? It seemed unlikely, because they were always fighting with one another. Why were they still together? It is because life is a comedy. Sometimes it feels like a bitter comedy. First it is bitter, and then later it becomes sweet.

The moon was full when the warrior returned home. He was covered in blood, but he had managed to win the battle. He and the other warriors took possession of the castle and celebrated by carousing and drinking immense quantities of wine. He was so happy that they were the winners. Everyone, he felt, must surely believe in them. Therefore he decided that he would reciprocally believe in everyone else. "I will do whatever the first person I meet tells me to do," he thought. He left the castle and walked down the road. After a mile he met a young man. "Hi," he said. "Hello," said the warrior.

Minutes with the Ground

January 25th, 1983. I wake up excited, utterly thrilled with this gift that is life. It's not like the excitement of Christmas morning a month ago. This is transcendent. This is the day when I will slip the surly bonds of earth; today I will fly in an airplane for the first time ever. I will walk in footless halls of air and reach out and touch the face of... (On those Island Tel commercials—reach out and touch someone—the face of the person on the phone would appear on the satellite dish at the top of the transmission tower, high in the sky.) In the window sharp white flakes are drifting dreamily through grey, as they always do at my happiest moments. My parents drive me to the Charlottetown airport, but I get on the plane alone and allow myself to be buckled in by a zephyr of perfume and fingernails that I assume must be one of the attendants of flight. I have my new Polaroid camera on my lap; it's like a lunchbox. I'm trying to hold it casually in hands that are already too big for my arms and body. I'm eleven. The flight adepts rove about closing compartments. I don't understand how they can be so nonchalant about what we are about to do. The impending miracle. Outside, the white flakes are now falling hard and fast from the grey shroud above, and I'm thrilled again by the thought that above the clouds the sun is shining. The demiurges of flight are moving around the plane in orange coveralls. The snowfall is turning to rain. I don't know it yet, but I won't be flying anywhere today. In 10 minutes, the captain will announce the regrettable but unavoidable cancellation, due to ice, of my first ever experience of flight. As I gaze at the wet sky, my stomach full of fluttering wings, I still don't realize that I'm grounded.

March 31st, 1999. It being a Wednesday, I walked to the junk store on Meadow Street and there I made an amazing discovery. In the pocket of a nice double-breasted suit I tried on there were four Polaroid photos: one of a woman lying on grass; one of the front of a dog; one of the tail of a dog, maybe the same one; and one of an unidentifiable stretch of ground, from an airplane. This is truly a miraculous find. I put them all back except the airplane photo.

April 1st. Today I thought about yesterday's discovery, which is sitting on my windowsill. After I thought about it for a while I realized what it is that makes it so interesting. Later I talked to Wendy on the phone for over an hour.

April 2nd. Today I reorganized my own photo collection. I picked out nine which are photos of the ground and another ten photos of the tops of clouds, all taken from airplanes. I taped them on the wall above my desk, and decided that they demonstrated a very deep-rooted truth.

Here's the true story of two brothers who loved each other very much. One day when they were both young they were skating on the pond and the younger brother fell in. He would have drowned but his older brother jumped in and saved his life, catching pneumonia in the process. After that he was an invalid for several years. Both brothers cursed gravity, which had caused the ice to break under the younger brother's weight. The younger brother built a printing press and started a newspaper at school which openly criticized the tyranny of gravity, under which all of their countrymen suffered. After school the brothers would meet up in the machine shed and invent new kinds of bicycles. Their resentment of gravity only increased when the older brother fell off his bicycle one day and broke his nose. It was a grudge that they would carry with them to adulthood. The brothers were insepar-able, they loved each other, they lived together and neither of them married. The only thing they lacked in their lives was a machine capable of engine-powered, manned, free flight. In bed at night they dreamed of ways that they could finally stick it to gravity, and help their country at the same time.

April 3rd. I made soup today with all the carrots in the bottom of the fridge. I asked Wendy what she thought about the airplane photos and she said she had seen many similar photos before. She also told me that she liked my installation of semi-functional television sets.

April 4th. When I got up today there was an unmarked envelope in my mailbox containing four photos of clouds taken from a plane. I was very excited by this anonymous artifact and immediately went to my desk to compare them to the photos I had taped up there. The comparison was extremely favourable. I stayed up quite late in my chair thinking about the implications, with Rosco asleep on my lap.

April 5th. I called Wendy and she confessed that she had been the one who put the envelope in my mailbox. Although I had feared this from the start, I found that my excitement was undiminished. I'm going to finish the carrot soup for lunch.

One day at a beach near Kitty Hawk, the two brothers tried out their new machine, the airplane. The younger brother steadied the wingtip while the older brother lay on the lower wing. After a 40-foot run the plane left the ground. Orville and Wilbur whooped and gave the finger to the planet Earth, and at that moment the brothers loved each other very much. Five years later, they had an army contract to make their machines for the good of the country. That was 1908. Today, these indomitable brothers are remembered as the visionary founders of the military-industrial complex. Their "airplane" is the second-deadliest weapon of the century. More than any other weapon before, it allows the attacker to safely distance himself from the people being killed. It is no match, however, for the most formidable weapon of all time, as Orville Wright discovered in 1908 when his plane crashed, injuring him and making his passenger the first fatality in the ongoing war between these two awesome weapons. The ground has always been and always will be the most effective blunt instrument in the history of warfare.

5 Minutes without the Ground

You never call. You never send me a card, a simple card. *I miss you more than you can guess / but I send you loads of happiness.* Nothing. No letters. No telegrams, smoke signals, pigeon deliveries. You said we'd keep in touch. I know I was the one who wanted more freedom. I know. But it was too hard to be always tethered down. I don't know which way is up anymore. I'm just floating around like a lonely electron. I see you every now and then, from far off. Why don't you ever call? Would that be so hard? A simple call?

The Meadow Street Alienation Society invites you to a frabjous community Day Without The Ground to celebrate the 100th anniversary of people leaving the ground and not coming back. The festivities will take place above the park. You are encouraged to come on stilts or suspended from helium-filled balloons. Bring a postcard. You are requested to donate your shoes to a good cause. Bring your pets. Please note that everything and everyone must be kept on a leash. Wear a name tag and bring a raincoat. Trampolines will be provided and yogic flyers are also welcome. Come in costume with an instrument. Excellent prizes. Meringue will be given away and large land mammals will be released into the wild blue yonder. Bring your camera. Amateur aerial photographers welcome. Callooh! Callay!

April 6th. Today there was something I was supposed to do for Wendy at the planetarium, but I thought I should stay home and make a list of idioms that involve the ground. The list is not exhaustive but I think it is a good "grounding" in the fundamentals (ha ha). Background, sacred ground, burial ground, ground zero. Ground coffee, ground water, grounds for divorce. Feet on the ground. (Head in the clouds.) I know Wendy will understand.

April 7th. Wendy brought her dog over and Rosco wouldn't come out from under the couch so we went for a walk in the park. It was a nice grey day and she wanted to take pictures. She has gathered some more photos for the collection; we now have around thirty. It's an impressive display. So far it's not clear what the point of these photos is.

April 8th. I realized today that using electricity at all in airplanes must be dangerous. The ground is also what allows electricity a safe means of escape.

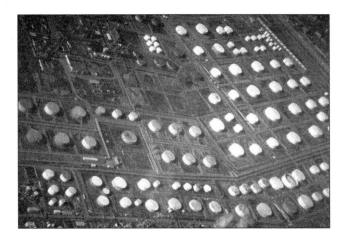

Edwin H. Land, in what year were you born? That was the
year after the first fatality due to an airplane crash, was it
not? And could you also please tell us the year of your
death? Which was the year of the Gulf War, wasn't it?
Thank you, Mr. Land. Your life has spanned a good part of
this century, and you have played no small part in the life
of the century as well, isn't that true? You invented many
optical devices such as the polarized filter? Have you ever
worked as a government advisor on guided missile tech-
nology? And were any of the projects you worked on ever
actually used in warfare? So it would be fair to say, then,
that your optical devices were essential to the develop-
ment of the guided missile? Thank you. Did you or did
you not invent the Polaroid camera, sometimes called the
Land camera? Could you describe to us, in layman's terms
please, what makes this camera different from other cam-
eras? Instantly, you say? Did I hear right? You don't have
to take the film to a film processing bureau? There's no

need to wait, then, for any length of time? I see. Mr. Land, I have here the instruction manual for your invention, the Polaroid camera. Do you recognize it? Mr. Land, what exactly is the real meaning of the phrase, "Stand at least three feet from your subject?" I remind you that you are under oath. Tell me, does absence, in your opinion, really make the heart grow fonder? Mr. Land, why would any-one—any reasonable person—have need of an instant photo of anything when the original remains right there in front of you? Mr. Land, wouldn't you say the Polaroid is the evolutionary apex of the camera? And doesn't it make reality redundant? Isn't the guided missile the essence of the airplane? And what would war be without pictures, anyway? Wasn't it always your plan, in fact, to orchestrate the merging of these technologies? Isn't it now possible to have an instant picture of whatever is on the ground at the very moment the missile hits? And isn't it beautiful? How far away should we stand, Mr. Land? Mr. Land?

April 9th. I was happy to read in the paper today that those stealth bombers were finally getting some use. A photo taken from a plane like that would really be something.

April 10th. I had decided to forget the airplane photos, but then I found another one. It's Saturday, of course, so I was overdue to go to the junk shop. This time I got serious and went through the drawers. This new photo is my favourite: it's black and white and seems old. I think it may have been taken during the war, actually. It makes me feel like Alice did after that poem: somehow it seems to fill my head with ideas—only I don't exactly know what they are! However, somebody killed something: that's clear, at any rate.

April 11th. I'm not sure the photos are important. It's time for a new project. It's difficult to find something to write about that everyone hates sufficiently that they will listen. When you write, you have to constantly figure out what it is that people hate the most, and even then you often have to remind them that they hate it. In any case, Wendy and I have had extensive discussions on the matter and I think we have figured out why it is that people take pictures of the ground from airplanes. Wendy said it must be nostagia. Nostalgia for what I asked. For the ground, she said. Yes, I said, that must be it.

April 12th. Went to my Earthquake-Preparedness class. On the way back I watched TV in a store window and a man in a white robe was just stepping down from an airplane. Then he bent down and gave the asphalt a kiss. I think the man was the Pope. Although I've never met the Pope.

The
Worthwhile
Flux

You're scared. Resentful. Angry. Your whole world is changing and you don't want to face it. You want yesterday again. Who will listen and really understand how scared and sick and angry you are?

"What with the war going on, I think it's not safe to fly," says the man obsessed with the Shroud of Turin as we leave Penn station. I was late getting on, and this was the last seat available. Why did no one else sit with him? It's hard to pinpoint, but obvious. The pocket of his white shirt is stuffed with leaky ball-point pens and small cardboard boxes. He twitches. Under his blue baseball cap his hair seems ready to explode. "But you know, it's a numbers game," he says. "Flying is a numbers game; the train is a numbers game. Everything is a numbers game." I don't know his name, but I know his origins. "I was born and raised in New York City," he tells me. "I like it here, but the rents are exuberant." Non-standard usage, one of my favourite things in the world. Like the pizza guy who had "Hurrocane" tattooed on his arm, or the sign at the clinic with the extra-potent, multipurpose quotation marks. "Do" "Not" "Ask" "How" "Long" "The" "Wait" "Will" "Be".

I'm leaving this jittery city after only four days. You're the reason I came, to be with you and our little euphemism. Don't you think it's hard to be subtle anymore? I want to tell the story like Hemingway does in "Hills Like White Elephants," but all our euphemisms and dysphemisms have gotten confused. The hills we pass—Catskills—are green, beautiful, and frankly, resemble hills. "I have something I want to show you," he says shortly after I sit down, and he produces a tattered 1970s *National Geographic* in a plastic slipcover, with the Shroud of Turin on the cover. He unfolds it to show me a smudged outline, supposedly left by Jesus' face. It's like a kindergarten art project. He doesn't say a thing, he just leafs through the pages, pointing and watching for my reaction. "It's proof," he says. I ask him, proof of what, and he gives me a look of pity. "Miracles can't be explained," he explains to me. "The reason miracles happen is not so that they can be explained. It's just so that they can be miracles." He gazes intently at the centrefold before putting it away. "Did you ever notice," he asks, as if nonchalantly, "that scientists always tell you what something is not, but they won't tell you what it is? They just want to tell you what it's not. With faith, though, you know. Some people, intellectuals, they don't want you to know anything. Everything is always changing; science is always changing. It's always in flux. But there's no point to it; it's not worthwhile, all this flux." After this he turns to the window and several minutes pass before he speaks again. "It's too much flux," he says.

On the train four days ago, I sat with a violin teacher who had wispy white hair and no eyebrows. I pretended to be asleep for a while, and one of the first things he said to me was that I looked like an angel while I slept. Later I woke up to find his hand on my thigh. I should travel by train more often, I thought to myself. It seems like I always meet very peculiar specimens of humanity. But then, perhaps humanity is more universally peculiar than I realized, and I just need to meet more people. In the seat in front of us now is a boy—or perhaps a girl, I'm really not sure—whose head is strangely shaped, a bit lemur-like. The boy/girl's behaviour set includes murmuring and keening, but his/her favourite activity is staring at me, with large eyes that seldom blink. She/he seems imperfectly formed, a mere doodle of a human being.

This is how big you were when you were only 11 weeks old. After that, you breathed, swallowed, digested, urinated, had bowel movements, slept, dreamed, woke, tasted, felt pain from touch and heat, reacted to light and noise, and were able to learn things.

There are no sign-wielding protesters outside the clinic, but there are some pamphlets scattered on the floor of the elevator. I know what they are before I look at them, so I stuff them in my pocket and don't show you. You've been fasting since midnight. You tell me how hungry you are as we pass through the metal detector. The waiting room is filled with women, alone or in pairs, and a couple of men flipping nervously through magazines. The carpet needs replacing, and all the chairs face the TV in the corner. The radio happens to be playing "Girls just wanna have fun," which we think is pretty true and it makes us laugh. "Three-fifty," says the woman at reception. I ask if a buffet is included in the price. She doesn't smile and neither do you. I feel inhibited by the tone of the room, which is pervasively unmirthful, and also by the conspicuousness of my Y-chromosome. The nurse calls out names—Vondelle, Desirée, Shaniqua—and one by one the women leave their sisters and friends and follow her through the door. Then she calls you, and when you're gone my mind tries desperately to distract itself with *Women's Health,* a large Fauvist mural about choice and respect, and the radio. Every pop song seems to be a tasteless joke, and I wonder if anyone else hears it. "Billie Jean is not my lover," insists the radio. "Only the good die young," it informs me. "How will I live without you?" it wants to know.

We skirt a lake, a mall, a military academy. My flux-saturated companion has ambiguous feelings about the war. "That's why I won't go on a plane, with all these people who call themselves terrorists. I remember in 1985 — did you see the news then? No? What happened was, there was a Palestinian terrorist on a ship, and a man of Jewish heritage was in a wheelchair, and the terrorist pushed him overboard. Right into the sea. I don't know how someone could do that. He just pushed his wheelchair right over. And this gentleman, this terrorist, has been hiding in Iraq." Lamely, I ask if he thinks that justifies bombing Iraqis. "Justifies?" He doesn't seem to know how to treat the word. "Was that justified, pushing that man into the sea?" I think he has missed my point, but then he says, "Killing can never be justified." He says it reproachfully, as if that's what I've been trying to do. "From the moment

of conception, life is sacred," he says. I wonder if he's been reading the same pamphlets I have. But then he adds as an afterthought, "Terrorists, though, they don't deserve life." The train has stopped at the border and customs officers are searching our bags, keeping us safe. They ask if I have any fruit, but I don't think they're hungry. Just outside my window three officers are standing around, wearing latex gloves. One has confiscated an apple, and they are all examining it closely, and laughing. I can't tell if it's the apple that's funny, or if the apple is just a prop. The joke may have nothing to do with the apple. It makes me feel nervous. For some reason, I am worried for that apple.

We know you are probably upset and confused. You are facing perhaps the greatest personal crisis of your life. You may feel guilt, anxiety, depression. This is what your feet looked like when you were only 10 weeks old. You even had fingerprints then. Please feel free to come out and talk with us. We are outside to listen and to help you.

While I'm waiting for you, I visit the restroom, for something to do. The back of the door is covered with disarmingly poignant graffiti: Terrell Loves Asha. Shireen Heart Michaelson. Marco and Jasmine Forever—Don't Hate. That last footnote is a puzzle to me. Have we become so hateful, that it's necessary to specifically request an exemption? When the women reappear, their faces are mostly unrevealing. No sign if it was only a test, or if some other euphemism is needed. They don't say anything to their friends. The blond woman who went in just before you comes out and barely glances at her boyfriend before they leave. I imagine what your face will look like: annoyed, distraught, your brow furrowed like it is sometimes. Suddenly I feel an ache, and a cartoon heart on my chest. When you finally come out, though, the expression on your face startles me. You look ill; you look afraid. "I want to leave," is all you say. The magnitude of the disaster is in your eyes, which won't meet mine. We can't have everything anymore, they say.

When the immigration officials ask me the purpose of my trip, I tell them I was visiting friends, but actually I only visited one, assuming that you're not plural. I considered telling my anti-terrorist acquaintance the true nature of my errand, so that I could watch for his reaction, but he has fallen asleep, and I've lost interest in provoking him because like every other person I've ever met, he reminds me of myself. "I used to think, you know, I didn't want to be involved in religion," he said to me. "I didn't believe in any religion. But it bothered me. The universe, I mean. Some people aren't bothered by it, but me, it bothered. Some people just don't think about it. A lot of people say, don't worry about it. The intellectuals, I mean. But I couldn't stop it bothering me, and I did a lot of thinking about it. And finally, I said, show me that you've got something. To God, I mean. I said to God, show me that you've got something to show. Prove to me that you exist."

He didn't look like he was going to continue, so in spite of myself I asked him. And? "And, He does. He does." So, I inquired, you had some kind of revelation at some point? "Yes. When I was very young." And then he was quiet, and suddenly he was sleeping. But the conversation had been worthwhile.

The lemur-like child is leaning over the seat again, eyes like searchlights. It would be unnerving, except that it seems to give her/him so much joy, to sit there looking at me, making noises like a bird. Why do I feel so much compassion for people on trains and buses and planes, where people are arguably at their worst? I can't read the newspaper on a plane, because no matter what the headlines are I become overwhelmed with pathos for the citizens of Earth below me, and how they are horrible and nice to one another all the time. It's an intensity particular to travel, I think. As though simple motion evokes the haphazard career of our lives from one catastrophe to another. If I am travelling to see someone, then on the train I am filled with a desire to connect with that person, to confess and reassure, to declare myself and make them believe. It's an emotional Doppler effect, feelings piling up on themselves and shifting my spectrum of behaviour as I draw near. On arrival, though, when I stop moving, my feelings quickly cool from red back to blue. Until I get back on the train to go home. Then I am reignited with inspiration, and I feel waves of regret that I didn't say what I wanted to say, or kiss who I wanted to kiss. Like my friend said, everything is always changing.

Believe in Yourself and Follow your Heart, says one of the pamphlets from the clinic, the one that addresses you as "Mom." I'm glad I didn't show them to you, not because they would make you feel guilty, but just because they want to make you feel guilty, and you get enough of that already. But I wish I had put my arm around you in the elevator. Everything is not gone for good, I should have said. It will come back. I told you once that my mood is always the same, but I lied. My mood is almost never the same; it's in constant flux too, between periods of serene lucidity when the world hits perfect notes, and periods of terrifying opacity when it seems deliberately and permanently off, and I am only a vague smudge on the fabric of my life, a smudge that doesn't prove anything. Two train events: Happy. Unhappy. Follow your heart, they say, but it's as though my heart is a piston: it pumps up and down, and the fluctuation is what drives me, what moves me from place to place. The downstroke gives power for the upstroke, which makes the flux worthwhile. Listen, you peculiar specimen of humanity, I want no more euphemism. Those hills, in winter, could indeed be white and elephantine. At 120 km/h it feels like I have this all figured out, but I can't guarantee it will last. If only it wasn't so hard to write on a train.

Simple Text

All Day I Dream About Sentences. I just walk around, inventing things to say to people. I don't smoke, but if someone gives me a cigarette I'll take it and put it in my mouth. Smoking makes your teeth yell-ow. I would like to play the cell-o. I am feeling rather mell-ow. *Quelqu'un a volé mon vél-o*. The reason I find it so hard to write poetry is that there are too many words to consider. For example, "otiose" and "sesquipedalian." What makes it worse is that a lot of the words I know happen to be both sesquipedalian and otiose. I think simple words are best, like "nice" or "pretty." Pretty is the best compliment I know how to give, because if something is pretty, that's enough. "Pretty" is a real word. The word "real" is too complicated. It's an otiose word.

At night, after dreaming about sentences all day, I lie in bed in the dark, with a notebook under my head so that sentences will dribble on to the page while I'm sleeping (the ones I'm self-conscious about saying while I'm awake). I suspect that there are some truly astonishing sentences in my head, but sometimes all I get is ear wax.

I've been in conversations with people and they say, "I know what you're going to say." But I haven't thought of what I'm going to say yet. It's embarrassing. They are thinking so much faster than I am; they can predict what I'm going to say before I have even thought of it. I have to try to anticipate what I'm going to say next. They say, "Go ahead. Say it. I know you're dying to say it." Meanwhile, my mind is racing. I have to come up with something, fast. I know that if I write enough sentences, eventually, all on their own they will evoke something I could never have dreamed of. And I have the feeling that, whatever it is, it will be extremely important. Perhaps it is more accurate to say, I want it to be important. But the fact that I want it to be important, this thing which has not yet been evoked, the fact that I am quietly passionate about its importance—that in itself is important.

As of now, I don't know what it will be, this thing that I'm going to say. But I have big ambitions for it. As I lie in bed, I dream about writing a powerfully incendiary text, which will incinerate all ordinary paradigms and ignite everyone it touches. Lurking under my bed is the uncreated conscience of my race, which I have accidentally forged in the smithy of my soul. It is growling ominously and threatening to leap out and devour the universe. The text that I dream of writing is a semiotic jack-hammer; it's a smart bomb; it's a runaway dildo; it's a vaccine against vacuous thought; it's an amendment to the constitution of the human psyche. It's a fantastic machine which will systematically dismantle society and then dismantle the world and then dismantle itself, and leave the pieces lying around in shuddering heaps on the ground, for anyone who comes along to pick up and take home.

It's a roller-coaster thrill-ride made entirely of toothpicks and spit. It's written in language as elusive and dangerous as a snuffleupagus with a taste for human flesh. It contains words, but they are words composed of elements previously unknown to science. It feeds your soul amphetamines and erects a *no vacancy* sign in the parking lot of your mind. It is so surprising that people say, whoa, is that a poem, or are you just happy to see me? The text I dream of writing is deceptively simple. It evokes the colour blue and takes us back to the childhood we never had. It's a lyric poem that won't stick to most dental work. It looks as though anyone could have written it, but there is a secret trick. It will induce a meditative alpha-state conducive to the occurrence of things you would never have thought possible, like truth and beauty. If I were to condense it into a single, epigrammatic phrase, it would say something simple and elegant and irrefutable, like: "My other car is an automobile." I dream of writing an epic one-liner, a one-liner so mind-blowingly pithy, which encapsulates the human condition so well, that it will be infinitely long, infinitely narrow, impossibly straight and true like the geometric definition of a line. Then the immense gravity of the next line I write will, in turn, alter the shape of reality, so that my stunning, infinitely succinct one-liner will curve, and the arc that it describes will be a miracle as meaningful as it is breath-taking. The text I dream of writing is a magical, wondrous, incredible thing.

However. The text I actually write always ends up being a rather modest construct, like a homemade birthday card.

My ability to communicate thought and feeling is both as immediate and as unreliable as breath. I trade in all this passion and what I get in return is something smaller and more efficient that comes with an instruction manual and has a tag that must not be removed under penalty of law. We must embrace and make the most of the globalization of text, say the representatives of major industrial countries. I'm an adult; I know the difference between fantasy and reality. Life is much easier now, thanks to advances in microbiology and text processing and distribution.

What I'm trying to say here is either so complex that it appears to be simple, or so incomprehensibly simple that you will never understand it unless I complicate things for you. Looking at the Earth from the surface of the Moon, all you see is a perfect blue-green marble. When, in fact, as you know, the Earth is a reasonably complicated place. What I'm trying to say is like that. Or else it is the opposite. But enough about me. I like your hair. Do you want a bowl of Jell-o?

It's Bits World

They were looking for a total transformation of mundane experience into bliss. It had become necessary. The winter came fast and hard, and it stayed a long time. The potatoes froze in the ground, there was not enough wood for the stove, and the modem was too slow. There was a war, and people were being asked to recycle aluminum. It was the off-season. I am so sleepy right now, but I'll tell you something: you should regard every anomaly as an opportunity to be awestruck.

When she was a small child she found a dead pigeon beside the railroad tracks, and later in the same place she found a dead calculator. Her friend went to the hospital. His cornea was wrinkled and it was making his eyelids stick together. It was the off-season. He closed up the shop and went out in search of a sandwich and a malted milk. "Oh God damn it for Christ's sake," he said. Love. What was this thing that so many poets made such a fuss about? When they first met, they stayed indoors all the time. He was agoraphobic and she was afraid to be alone.

In those days everyone had a story to tell. Losing a toe to frostbite or getting one's head stuck in a milkcan. Outside, the streets were dirty and cold. They needed distraction. They wanted to see everything, so they would be distracted from everything else. He is a man in fine fettle. He possesses a generous spirit, and she has nice manners. She knew when she got up that morning it would not be an ordinary day. They took a lot of things with them: it was not the things they were trying to escape so much as the origins of things. They had to forget where ideas came from in order to find them interesting again. She justified the trip as "radical chemotherapy for my cancerous soul."

All the hotels were filled with celebrities they didn't know. People were eating their dinners alone in restaurants. The mountains were dream-like and seemed smaller than she had imagined. On the side of the highway there were farmers selling Kool-aid. The amusement park employees were not amused. Of all the rides, the bus back to the city was the one they liked most. There was a restaurant that served nothing but insects, and another one that served only tofu. "Can you drive a standard?" he asked. They drove a Chevy to the levee and drove a Ford to the fjord. They tried to make themselves more interesting by being interested in more things. Some of the maps had to be stretched to make them fit. "You can't get there from here," he said. "It seems like I can't even get *here* from here," she replied.

Everywhere they went, the souvenirs had been made somewhere else. "There are so many beautiful places in the world," she said. "But they are so disorganized." They couldn't picture themselves in any tragic news reports, so when the boat was overcrowded and barely out of the water, they didn't complain. The hotel room was exactly six feet long by three feet wide by three feet high, and it had a TV. Oh, I'm so drowsy. What should we do? Let's go for a stroll by the river, for a change of pace. Do you want to see a movie? It seems silly to go to a movie theatre. They called home and left messages for themselves. When they found an internet café they digitized postcards and emailed them to friends. Tourism is the greatest gift of the twentieth century, they thought. "The reason I'm always having fun," she said, "is that I'm doing what I like. I'm the happiest loser alive," she said. "My specialty is nonchalance," he said.

Ten miles out of the city they saw the most amazing sight they had ever seen. A lifetime of unspoken, unconscious supplication was finally rewarded. They were late getting back to the train station and the train was already beginning to pull away. They called out for it to stop so they could get on. The conductor asked, "Do you have tickets? Who are you?" New man, new woman, feeling lucky to be somehow caught up in this tedious, cruel, and inexplicable existence. New woman, new man, carrying an old suitcase with 30 lbs. of brandy-filled chocolates and no spare underwear. Reading books upside-down and backwards. Losing our wallets with a sense of purpose. Sleeping with our eyes open. Haggling over hagiography, canonizing cartoon characters. Boxing with St. Goofy. Paying for dinner with underarm deodorant. Leaving a trail of discarded punctuation marks. Taking out insurance and releasing it into the wild. Fucking on the carpet, between the seats. "I am a gentle philosopher of the road," he proclaimed. "I am the zeitgeist multiplied by a weltschmerz," she declared. New man and new woman, picking up the pieces and moving on, except sideways this time.

They played Scrabble in the observation car, by moonlight, with blankets around them and strangers sleeping in the corners. They passed a frozen waterfall. They found a newspaper and discovered that there had been an election while they were gone. The war had moved on to a different part of the world. The stars fizzled and went out. The leaves were vivid in a way that made them feel lightheaded. Sunrise above the clouds doesn't compare with this, he admitted. "It's so... ineffable!" she exclaimed. "That exclamation mark," he said. "That exclamation mark is the last exclamation mark you'll ever need."

Two people are travelling on a train. Watching tiny villages and fields go by, having sex in the washroom. "It's bits world," she says. It's bits world. Let's get along with me. I am an edifying and enjoyable text-based performance artist, and this is the most comfortable performance you have ever run into. Wherever you may be, whoever you are, when you think of usefulness, think of Bits.

Notes

Some of these texts have previously appeared in other publications: A Few Advanced Yo-yo Tricks in *Blood & Aphorisms* (Experimental issue, 2000). Summer Plum (Winter Version) in *The Walrus* (1:6, July 2004). 5 Minutes with the Communist Manifesto in *Short Fuse: The Global Anthology of New Fusion Poetry* (New York: Rattapallax, 2002). V: The Miniseries in audio form on the CD *Millennium Cabaret* (Wired on Words, 1998). Everything I Know About Aphids in *Blood & Aphorisms* (Mont Real issue, 2000) and on the CD accompanying *Short Fuse*. It's Bits World in *Narrativity 2* (2001). Also, Communist Manifesto, Acadian Bus Lines, and With/out the Ground appeared in the chapbook *Tonight you'll have a filthy dream* (Backwards Versions 2, 1999), while Yo-yo, Aphids, Bits, Simple, and Quotations appeared in *I feel perfectly fine* (Backwards Versions 3, 2000). These self-published chapbooks, along with Backwards Versions 1, *Three Odd Numbers* (1999), collected the performance pieces I'd done in Montreal between 1992 and 2000. Only 50 or so copies were made of each. Many of these pieces have also been recorded for my CD *Bits World: Exciting Version*, and all have been well-enunciated on stage.

In other words, this book represents about a decade of talking at people and trying to ignore them if they talk back; a decade of talking backwards into numerous microphones. These pieces were first performed: A Few Advanced Yo-yo Tricks at Quai des Brûmes on St.Denis (29/04/00), at a benefit for Montreal's Anarchist Book Fair. Instructional slides and a cassette tape were employed. Summer Plum (called Summer Poem at first) at the Sala Rossa on St. Laurent during the first Festival Voix D'Amériques (01/02/02). 5 Minutes with the Communist Manifesto at Bistro 4 on St. Laurent for the launch of the *Millennium Cabaret* CD (22/11/98)—Francesca operated the timer—and then at a special Commie-Red edition of Jake Brown's YAWP (23/01/99). In Quotations / Out of Context at Cabaret Music Hall (St. Laurent) in a show benefitting Santropol Roulant (13/11/99). V: The Miniseries was recorded on a minidisc in Japan in 1996. Everything I Know About Aphids at a two-day Spoken Word Festival at Concordia University (21-22/09/99). 5 Minutes with the Global Economy at MAI (Jeanne-Mance) during the first Solofest (02/11/00). Acadian Bus Lines at the very intimate Galerie Fokus, on Duluth, way back in

(02/95). Stories That Don't Explain Anything in Nichols 109, at Bishop's University's English Language Summer School, Level One (25/05/04). 5 Minutes with/without the Ground at the extremely intimate Yellow Door, on Aylmer, with a Polaroid camera in my hands (08/04/99). Simple Text at the Jailhouse on Mont-Royal (17/11/00), in aid of Vincent Tinguely and Victoria Stanton's really worthwhile documentary project *Impure: Reinventing the Word*. It's Bits World at the launch of Lance Blomgren's *Walkups* at Casa del Popolo on St. Laurent (17/10/00). And all of these, many times since. A Farewell to Q and The Worthwhile Flux, both written in 2004, were first performed not in Montreal but abroad, in the UK, South Africa, and Australia, and the details are not a part of this chronicle.

The photos in this book were all taken by Corey Frost with these exceptions: p.29, most likely taken by Sidney Frost (the subjects are, I believe, Stanley Carr and Robert Frost); p.66 (C. Frost at a Beppu sunaburo) and p.127 (Smokey's shadow on the bridge to PEI) by Cynthia Quarrie; and p.139 (White Sands, NM) by Karen Weingarten. The front cover photo is a sunrise over Sept-Iles, QC, from a Dash-8. Other locations: p.12: traffic-safety dinosaur in Ochiai-cho. p.14: Golden Gate Bridge, CA. p.18: Carlsbad Caverns, NM. p.24: Coney Island, NY. p.26: a helicopter. p.27: a boy and his seal. p.32: Himeji-jo. p.61: pizza joint in Saijo-cho. p.64: cherry blossoms at Himeji castle. p.70: apartments in Seoul. p.71-73: Las Vegas, NV. p.74: movie poster in Japan. p.78: mill in Sept-Iles. p.80: Quebec, Summit of the Americas, 2001. p.87: Manhattan Bridge, from the Brooklyn side. p.90: Manitoba. p.96: National Museum, Jakarta. p.98: Scotland. p.100: constitutional referendum Oct., 1995. p.101: on the "John Lennon wall" in Prague. p.102: Gardiner Expressway, Toronto. p.107: Bryce Canyon, UT. p.109: unknown city on the St. Lawrence. p.110: over Mt.Fuji. p.115: somewhere in QC. p.116: Mile-End tracks. p.119: Scotland, near Tongue. p.120: Hong Kong. p.123: Austrian parliament, Vienna. p.132: picture on the wall in a cruddy hotel in Trieste. p.134: Northeast of Brazil. p.144: C. Frost, in Kuse-cho.

I feel that acknowledgement of influence in these pieces is owed to the following entities and items: *Adbusters* magazine, Adidas sportswear, Louis Althusser, America's Funniest Home Videos, Roland Barthes, Gary Barwin, Jorge Luis Borges, George Brecht, André Breton, Lewis Carroll, the Children's

Television Workshop, Richard Henry Dana Jr., Fluxus, C.C. and S.M. Furnas (authors of *The Story of Man and his Food*), Sheila Heti, Ray Johnson, Andy Kaufman, Robert Kroetsch, Kronos Quartet, V. I. Lenin, Marx and Engels, Anne Michaels, Malcolm Morley, Eileen Myles, Pavement, Alain Robbe-Grillet, the San-X Co. of Japan, Robert Paul Smith (author of *Time and the Place*, subtitled "He Led a Double Life"), Stereolab, The Terminator movies, V: The Miniseries, Orson Welles, Oscar Wilde, William Carlos Williams, Orville and Wilbur Wright, Xena Warrior Princess, and Banana Yoshimoto. I'm not very picky. This list has influences too, and the definitive version would be an infinitely recursive *mise-en-abîme*.

Many others deserve at least a firm handshake from these notes, but any attempt to be comprehensive is certain to fail. Thanks to all those people and institutions who have hosted me and/or my performances in their cities, and/or who have been helpful along the way. In particular, thanks of diverse kinds to Patchen Barss, Tracy Bohan, Jake Brown, Colin Christie, Julie Crysler, Alison Darcy, Ian Ferrier, Dave Ainsworth and Maeve Haldane, Catherine Kidd, Jim Munroe, Margaret Schnipper, Gail Scott, Victoria Stanton, Todd Swift, Vince Tinguely, and my grumpily indulgent editor, Andy Brown. Also thanks to the Canada Council for the Arts, for its support of this press and my writing.

In the time during which these texts were written, several people who had a marked influence on me have died. My father's mother and my mother's father: I loved and admired them both and obviously this whole endeavour would never have been possible without them. And four writers who inspired me immensely all died too soon: first Ian Stephens, then Kathy Acker, then Edward Saïd, then Spalding Gray. There is so much tragedy in that short epitaph that the world seems a dramatic place indeed, and the ways they struggled with it seem heroic.

Lastly and most resoundingly, certain people deserve special mention for their contribution, voluntary or not, to these texts: my mother, for the milkcan incident; Michy and Rei and Yuta; Cynthia Quarrie, who will have to change her name; Alum whom I met on a plane; others whom I met on trains and buses; Jennifer Westlake and Django; Elissa Jiji for dancing at a wake with me; Dana Bath from Snail Cove; my 2004 Level One ELSS class and all my other students; and Karen H. Weingarten, who is somehow both nice and pretty. Mayonnaise.